THE·PARENT·AND·CHILD
·PROGRAMME·

Dinah Dragon's
Busy Day

Jane Salt

Illustrated by Rebecca Elgar

KT-162-082

Series editor **Penni Cotton**
Senior Lecturer, Reading and Language Studies
Kingston Polytechnic

To Parents

By sharing books together at home you can play a vital part in helping your child learn to read. This series is designed to give the right support to your child in the early stages of reading — so that you can read together with confidence and enjoyment.

How to read this book together

▷ Make reading together a comfortable and special time.

▷ Introduce the story by talking about the character on page 5. Your child may have met this character in other books in the *Parent and Child Programme*.

▷ **You, as the Storyteller, read the words at the bottom of the page marked with this symbol.**

▷ **After you have read your part, ask your child to join in with the words in the speech bubbles**. All these bubble words are repeated from the words you have just read.

▷ Point to the words in the bubbles as they are read.

▷ On the first reading you could read the story and the first few bubbles yourself so your child thoroughly understands the idea before joining in.

Remember young children love repetition — and the more they read a story the more confident they will feel about joining in or reading their words alone.

Always use the pictures as they give lots of clues. Talk about what the characters are doing and encourage your child to predict what is going to happen next.

If your child is stuck just give the word yourself. This is far more helpful than sounding out individual letters.

Always praise good guesses — much of the skill in reading is in guessing or predicting what the word will be.

Always end reading together on a positive note.

"I hate housework," said Dinah Dragon.

5

"Who will help me? " she asked.

"I will," said Declan Dragon and
Desmond Dragon together.

"I will," said Dizzie Dragon.

8

So all the dragons put on their
aprons, ready to help.

9

"Who will help me wash the dishes?"
asked Dinah Dragon.

10

"I will," said Declan Dragon.
"I'm good at washing up."

11

"Oh dear!" he said, "I've had a
little accident."

12

"Never mind," said Dinah
(who was a patient dragon).

13

"Who will help me dust?" asked Dinah Dragon.

14

"I will," said Dizzie Dragon.
"I'm good at dusting."

15

"Oh dear!" said Dizzie. "We've had a little accident."

16

"Never mind," said Dinah
(who was a very patient dragon).

17

"Who will help me clean the carpet?"
asked Dinah Dragon.

18

"I will," said Desmond Dragon.
"I'm good at cleaning."

19

"Oh dear!" said Desmond. "I've had a little accident."

20

"Never mind," said Dinah (who
was a very, very patient dragon).

21

But she looked a bit sad.

It seemed as if her house would never
be tidy.

Declan Dragon, Dizzie Dragon
and Desmond Dragon looked at
all the mess.

24

"Time for magic!" they said.

So they twirled and they swirled…

...and twitched their tails...

… and the house was sparkling clean.

"Thank you," said Dinah Dragon.

"That's what I call magic."